DORIN
and the DRAGON

by ARIANE DEWEY

GREENWILLOW BOOKS, New York

The art was prepared as a black pencil and wash
drawing with color overlays for red, yellow, and blue.

31690

Library of Congress Cataloging in Publication Data
Dewey, Ariane.   Dorin and the dragon.
Summary: Disinherited by his father, a young prince
wanders from country to country until he stops at
a castle inhabited by a friendly blind dragon.
[1. Fairy tales. 2. Folklore—Greece] I. Title.
PZ8.D498Do   398.2'2'0938 [E]   81-6850
ISBN 0-688-00910-7   AACR2
ISBN 0-688-00911-5 (lib. bdg.)

Long ago there was a king who had three sons. One evening he said to his sons, "When you awake in the morning, come and tell me what you saw while you slept."

In the morning all three arose early and appeared before their father. The eldest son spoke first. "Father," he said, "I dreamed I held cities in my hands. They were filled with workers and they were surrounded by rich green fields and pastures of fat sheep."

"A princely dream," said the king. "I will give you that part of my kingdom which you saw in your dream."

The second son said, "How strange! I had the same dream as my brother."

"Good," said the king. "You too shall have farmlands, sheep and cities.

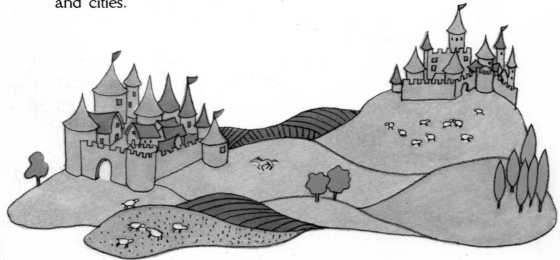

 ow Dorin, what did you dream?" the king asked his youngest son.

"Oh, Father, I'm afraid my dream will anger you," said the prince.

"I must hear it anyway," insisted the king.

"In my dream, Father, you brought me a bowl and poured water into it so I could wash, then you dried my hands with a towel."

"What!" shouted the king. "You dare see me as your servant! I see that your fortune lies elsewhere!" And he banished Dorin from the kingdom forever.

or months Dorin wandered from country to country. One day, tired and hungry, he stopped at a castle, but when he went inside, he found only some empty pails lying about. There was no food and he saw no one.

Soon however, he heard a thunderous noise. Into the courtyard marched a huge dragon leading a thousand sheep! Dorin was terrified, but the dragon paid no attention to him. He milked the sheep, drank the contents of each and every pail, and sat down to smoke.

The dragon was blind. When Dorin saw this, he said quietly, "Father, your son is home."

"What son?" said the dragon. "I have no son, but if you can take a blow from my tail, I will call you son."

Dorin quickly stuffed a sack with straw, placed it near the dragon and lay down against a wall out of the dragon's reach.

"Ready," he called.

The dragon swung his tail around and around. He struck the sack which burst, scattering straw all over.

"Well, are you alive?" the dragon asked.

"Yes, Father."

"That's good," said the dragon. "Now, my son, you must be my eyes since I am blind."

"Gladly, Father," said Dorin.

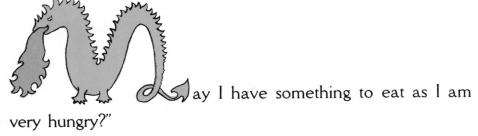

ay I have something to eat as I am very hungry?"

"I only drink milk," said the dragon, "but take this wand, wave it and you will have food. Wave it again when you have finished and what is left will vanish."

Dorin ate heartily and waved away the dirty dishes.

hen the dragon took his sheep to graze, Dorin explored the castle. There was much to see. One morning in a forgotten corner he found a flute. He played it and everything began to dance. The stools danced with the pails, the table with the chairs, the carpets bounced up and down, everything danced. Dorin looked out the window and saw the trees on the hill, the horses, the birds and the flowers in the fields all dancing. It made him so dizzy that he put the flute away in his pocket.

The next morning he said to the dragon, "Let me take the sheep today, Father, so you can stay home and rest."

"All right," said the dragon, "but stay away from the highest hill. Wicked dryads live there. They watch for travelers, to steal their eyes. Many years ago they tricked me and stole my eyes because I warned travelers away."

Dorin assured the dragon that he would not go near the dryads' hill. But once outside, he drove the sheep straight to the highest pasture where the grass was thick and tall and sweet. The sheep grazed till they were tired and their udders were filled with milk. Dorin climbed a tree to watch over them.

Looking down from their castle window, one of
the dryads discovered the prince in the tree. "Come, sisters," she
called, "and see the treat we will have today."

They rushed out to capture Dorin, but he saw them com-
ing and began to play his flute. At once everything danced—
the sheep, the grass, the trees and, of course, the dryads.

Come here, come to us," they sang, leaping high in the air around the tree trying to reach Dorin. As one of the dryads jumped up, Dorin grabbed her by the hair and twisting it around a branch, hung her up like a bunch of grapes. When her sisters tried to rescue her, they met the same fate.

"Let us down and we will grant whatever you wish," they pleaded.

"Give me the eyes of the dragon and I will untie you," Dorin said.

"We will as soon as you set us free."

"No," said Dorin, "tell me where my father's eyes are and when I have them, I'll set you free."

n our castle you will find two demons cooking supper," said the dryads. "Be sure not to say 'boo' or you will scare them away. Just say 'chuck, chuck' and ask them to get the two golden apples from the top shelf. Then hurry back and get us down!"

Dorin guessed it was a trick so when he entered the castle, instead of saying "chuck, chuck," he shouted "BOO" so loudly that the startled demons fell into the fire. He took the golden apples from the shelf, returned to his sheep and herding them together left for home, leaving the dryads hanging in the tree.

"My father will get you down when he has his eyes back," Dorin called.

s soon as Dorin returned, the dragon began milking his sheep. "In all my years I have never gotten so much milk. Where did you graze these sheep?" he asked in amazement.

"I can see where the grass is greenest and take the herd there."

"I would give anything to see again," said the dragon sadly as he settled down to drink his milk.

"Here, Father, is an apple for dessert," Dorin said.

"I don't like apples, you eat it," grumbled the dragon.

"I've been eating apples all afternoon. Just taste this one."

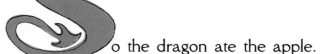o the dragon ate the apple.

"I can see!" he shouted. "I can see with my left eye!" he cried and leaped about in excitement.

"Eat another, Father, and you will see with your right eye, as well!"

The dragon swallowed the second apple whole and at once saw with both eyes. He embraced Dorin and said, "All I have I will share with you, but my wealth does not compare with your gift to me!"

Then Dorin told the dragon how he had fooled the dryads. "And they are still hanging on the tree," he added.

"I know what to do about that!" the dragon said. They returned to the tree. One breath of dragon-fire and the dryads were no more.

The dryads were gone and the country was safe.

he dragon, now that he had his eyes back, could not have enough of looking. First he showed Dorin every nook and cranny of their kingdom, and then they set out to see the world.

7